For Lucca, the true author behind this tale. —G.K.
For Bernardo and Arthur, purveyors of high-decibel entertainment. —E. M. B. B.

Translated from the Portuguese by Eric M. B. Becker
First English language Edition published in North America in 2022 by Tapioca Stories
English language edition © 2022 Tapioca Stories
English translation © 2022 Eric M. B. Becker
Text and illustrations © 2017 Guilherme Karsten
Originally written under the title *Aaahhh!*
Translation rights arranged through the VeroK Agency, Barcelona, Spain

Library of Congress Control Number: 2021945185
ISBN: 978-1-7347839-2-6

MIX
Paper from
responsible sources
FSC® C144853
FSC
www.fsc.org

Printed in China
First Printing, 2022

TAPIOCA
STORIES

© 2022 Tapioca Stories
55 Gerard St. #455, Huntington, New York 11743
www.tapiocastories.com

Guilherme Karsten

TAPIOCA
STORIES

A minute ago,
this was the tallest
mountain in the world ...

... *was* ... a minute ago.

A minute ago, there was only
the North Pole and the South Pole.

... *was* ... a minute ago.

A minute ago, this was the biggest tiger in the world ...

... *was* ... a minute ago.

Now it is the biggest *stripeless* tiger in the world.

Planet Earth has been taken over
by a very noisy noise. So noisy that
some people have been left deaf,
and others with a stutter.

The music of the radio is drowned
out by the roaring sound. The blast
has sent cars, animals, and bystanders
flying left and right!

Supercomputers with mega-powers and a million flashing lights are working to trace the source of the noise. Meanwhile, the piercing sound launches fierce tidal waves and rouses sleeping volcanoes.

Scientists have used super satellites with telescopes and thousands of shock waves to confirm it is not an alien invasion.

To everyone's surprise, the earsplitting ruckus seems to be coming from right here on Planet Earth.

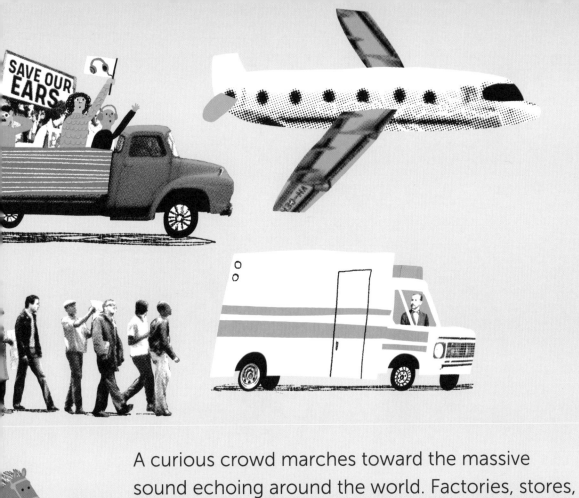

A curious crowd marches toward the massive
sound echoing around the world. Factories, stores,
and even schools close their doors (making some
children quite happy).

Something really BIG is going on!

Trucks with sonic radars and thousands of
dazzling buttons lead the way. But where is
the giant noise coming from?

It looks like we're getting close to the source
of this overwhelming sound. What do you
think we'll find?

A meteor crashing into
a foghorn factory?

A saxophone playing out of tune?
No, not one—a thousand saxophones?

What could it be? Any guesses?

"Easy there, Son, this won't hurt at all. Scream any louder and the neighbors will hear!"

"Wow, Papa, I had no idea we had so many neighbors!"